Ballet Stories

Retold from the classic originals
by Lisa Church

Illustrated by Eric Freeberg

STERLING

New York / London

www.sterlingpublishing.com/kids

STERLING and the distinctive Sterling logo
are registered trademarks of Sterling Publishing Co., Inc.

Library of Congress Cataloging-in-Publication Data

Church, Lisa R., 1960–
  Ballet stories / retold by Lisa Church ; illustrated by Eric Freeberg.
     v. cm. — (Classic starts)
  Summary: Retells eight ballet plots based on original and classic fairy tales.
  Contents: Cinderella—The sleeping beauty—Coppélia—Swan Lake—The
little mermaid—The ugly duckling—The firebird—The nutcracker.
  ISBN 978-1-4027-6663-3
  1. Fairy tales. [1. Fairy tales. 2. Ballets—Stories, plots, etc.] I. Freeberg, Eric, ill.
II. Title.
  PZ8.C47Bal 2010
  [E]—dc22

                                                                    2009007158

Lot#:
2 4 6 8 10 9 7 5 3 1
11/09
Published by Sterling Publishing Co., Inc.
387 Park Avenue South, New York, NY 10016
Text © 2010 by Lisa Church
Illustrations © 2010 by Eric Freeberg
Distributed in Canada by Sterling Publishing
$^{c}/o$ Canadian Manda Group, 165 Dufferin Street
Toronto, Ontario, Canada M6K 3H6
Distributed in the United Kingdom by GMC Distribution Services
Castle Place, 166 High Street, Lewes, East Sussex, England BN7 1XU
Distributed in Australia by Capricorn Link (Australia) Pty. Ltd.
P.O. Box 704, Windsor, NSW 2756, Australia

Classic Starts is a trademark of Sterling Publishing Co., Inc.

Printed in China
All rights reserved

Sterling ISBN 978-1-4027-6663-3

For information about custom editions, special sales, premium and
corporate purchases, please contact Sterling Special Sales
Department at 800-805-5489 or specialsales@sterlingpublishing.com.

CONTENTS

∽

CHAPTER 1

Cinderella

⌒

Once upon a time, there lived a girl who sparkled with loveliness. Her heart was as big as her smile, and her actions showed kindness and gentleness to all.

However, when her father remarried, she was forced to live with her new stepmother, Betty, and two stepsisters, Darlene and Della. It was then she learned that not all girls were kind like her.

"Do the dishes! Sweep the floor! Make our beds! Now do some more!" the two sisters and their mother would chant. They were so unkind to the girl! They even called her Cinderella, because after her housework was finished, they would send her to rake the cinders in the kitchen fireplace.

When the day was done, Cinderella would go to her bed of straw exhausted from her long hours of work. Her stepsisters would go to their rooms, where their beds were made of the softest feathers. They would look in their mirrors that reached from ceiling to floor, thinking of no one but themselves. Yet no matter how badly Cinderella was treated, she was always sweet and helpful.

One day, the prince of the kingdom sent out invitations for a grand ball. It was time he chose a wife. All the ladies of the land were invited. Some of the important men of the kingdom were invited, too.

The stepsisters nearly burst with excitement.

In the days leading up to the party, they chattered of nothing else.

"I want to wear my red velvet gown. It is trimmed with lace and pearls," said Darlene in a dreamy state.

"Fine!" said Della. "Though I will be much prettier in my blue silk dress. It has a gold pattern and is studded with diamonds!"

The two argued about their gowns until Cinderella piped up. They finally stopped bickering when the forgotten girl promised to give each of them a new hairstyle for the ball. The sisters accepted this offer. In fact, they expected it, for Cinderella did everything for them.

For the next several days, Cinderella wasn't only busy with her usual housework. She also ironed skirts and fluffed ruffles and stitched hems. Of course, neither of the two sisters offered a thank-you for her help.

"Cinderella, wouldn't *you* love to be going to

the ball?" teased Della when the big night finally arrived.

The girl looked down at her outfit of rags. A light frown swept across her face.

"It would be a dream," she said softly. "But it is not meant to be. I have no time to get ready, nor do I have a dress. This night is meant for ladies of fashion, like you. So hurry along. You shouldn't keep the prince waiting."

"For once you are right, Cinderella," Darlene answered in a snobbish voice. "People would laugh seeing a cinder-maid like you at a ball!"

The young girl's stepmother entered the room just as the coach pulled up to the house. "Time to go, girls! Cinderella, *do* make use of your time while we are away. You are behind on the washing and ironing, and I think the kitchen floor should be done again. It is not nearly shiny enough. Sometimes I think you are worthless!"

The stepmother's words stung the poor girl

like a wasp. Cinderella felt the tears run down her cheeks as she watched the mean woman and her daughters ride off toward the king's castle. She walked out the front door and longingly looked at their fancy coach headed to the palace.

Feeling sorry for herself was not something the young girl usually experienced, but tonight she allowed a little self-pity into her heart. How she wished she could flitter through the ballroom, slow-dance with the prince, and taste the delicious food! She put her head in her hands and cried.

Perhaps Cinderella's desire to attend the ball was so strong that it created magic. Perhaps someone special was looking out for her. Whatever the reason may have been, at that moment something magical happened. Something more wonderful than Cinderella had ever dreamed possible.

BALLET STORIES

In a breeze from above, a magical woman appeared out of nowhere. She was dressed in a beautiful white gown. A glittering wand swayed gracefully in her hand.

"Cinderella, I am your fairy godmother. Why do you cry, my dear? What is wrong?" The soft voice startled the young girl. Nobody had ever spoken to her so kindly before.

"Oh," whispered Cinderella. "I, uh . . . I wish . . ."

"I know," said her fairy godmother. "I have been watching you. You wish you could go to the ball. I say, my beauty, I don't blame you. I rather wish I could go myself!"

The pretty girl gave a tiny smile then lowered her eyes once again.

"My beautiful one, you wish to go to the royal ball? Then you shall," said her fairy godmother. "I will get you to the ball! Now dry your eyes and do exactly as I say."

Cinderella wiped away her tears, not really believing what she was hearing. But she stood still and listened to what she was told.

"Run to the garden, my dear, and bring me the biggest pumpkin you can find!"

Cinderella raced to the garden and returned with a beautiful orange pumpkin. She wondered how it would help her get to the ball. Her fairy godmother touched it with her wand and turned it into a lovely golden carriage.

"Now we need some horses," said her fairy godmother. "Please bring me the mousetrap from the kitchen pantry."

Cinderella gave her a smile and was back in a flash with a cage that held six little gray mice. At the touch of the wand, the furry little creatures became dapple-gray horses, ready to lead the carriage.

"But what shall we do for a coachman?" asked Cinderella. "Who will drive me to the ball?"

"A rat would do most nicely," said her fairy godmother.

Cinderella once again ran off, promising to bring back exactly what the beautiful fairy had asked for.

"Here is a rat!" Cinderella announced proudly.

Once again, with a touch of the wand, magic happened. The rat became a splendid coachman. He wore a black suit quite perfect for formal events.

"And last," her fairy godmother said, "we need footmen. Six lizards should do. Look in the garden behind the watering can."

By this time, Cinderella was so excited she could hardly keep track of what she was doing. "Lizards, lizards," she repeated to herself. While looking around the garden, she found them right behind the watering can and scooped them up. Cinderella ran all the way back to her fairy godmother with the slippery little reptiles cupped in her hands.

"You are footmen!" her fairy godmother announced as she touched each one softly with the wand. Every new man jumped up and ran to the carriage, looking as though he'd had the job forever.

"And now, my sweetness, it is time to go. Are you ready for the ball?" The fairy gazed at the girl with bright eyes.

Cinderella's smile turned into a frown. She looked down, touching her ragged dress.

"I can't go like this," she said with a sigh.

Before Cinderella could think of how messy she looked, her fairy godmother waved her wand again. A sprinkle of pink glitter and fog surrounded her. Cinderella was now dressed in a gown of beautiful gold and silver silk. The edges were studded with pearls and precious gems. On her feet were the most delicate pair of

crystal shoes, small enough to fit only a dainty girl like her.

"Cinderella," said her fairy godmother, "your carriage awaits, and you look beautiful. But I must tell you this: At the stroke of midnight, this wonderful dream must come to an end. Your carriage will turn back into a pumpkin, your horses will become mice, and the footmen will once again be lizards. And this glorious dress, unfortunately, will change back into the rags you wore before."

Cinderella promised to return well before midnight. She stepped into the magical carriage, which carried her off to the grand ball.

When Cinderella reached the palace, word spread that a beautiful princess had arrived. The prince came out to her carriage to meet her, and he led her into the ballroom.

As they entered the room, the entire place froze. The musicians stopped playing, the guests stopped dancing, and every person was curious about who this lovely princess could be. The guests began whispering. The king even told the queen he hadn't seen any lady this lovely in years, Her Majesty excluded, of course.

The prince led Cinderella through the crowd of guests to the dance floor. They moved into the center where everyone could see them. They danced there for the entire evening.

At eleven o'clock, a delicious dinner was served. Cinderella happened to be seated beside her nasty stepmother and stepsisters. They didn't even recognize her. Cinderella talked to them as though she were a lady of society, not a cinder-maid.

As midnight drew closer, Cinderella remembered her promise to her fairy godmother. She curtsied to the king and queen and accepted their invitation to come back to the next evening's ball. The prince then walked her to her carriage and said good night. He stood and watched as she rode away.

When Della, Darlene, and their mother returned home that night, they could not stop talking about the party. Cinderella's stepmother left so the girls could gossip among themselves.

"You should have seen the princess at the ball, Cinderella!" Della said.

"She was the loveliest girl I've ever seen!" added Darlene. "The prince was quite taken with her." Cinderella blushed at their words, wondering how they would feel if they knew they were talking about her.

"Oh, perhaps I can go tomorrow night!" said Cinderella excitedly.

Della laughed loudly. "A girl like you doesn't belong at a ball."

Cinderella's stepmother came back into the room. "The second night of the ball is tomorrow, but now it's time for sleep. My daughters, go to bed! Cinderella, finish cleaning the kitchen. It doesn't look like you've done a thing in there tonight."

The next evening, Cinderella's fairy godmother made another secret visit. She touched Cinderella with her wand, and transformed her just as she had the night before. The girl became even more beautiful. Cinderella's fairy godmother prepared the coach, horses, and footmen to take her to the ball.

"Be home before midnight!" her fairy

godmother called as Cinderella rode away in her carriage.

The prince again spent a whirlwind evening of dancing and dining with his lovely princess. They enjoyed their time together so much that the hours passed by quickly. Cinderella lost track of the time. Before she knew it, the clock began to strike twelve. Only then did she remember her fairy godmother's warning.

Running for the door, she looked back at the prince. She tried to memorize the face she might never see again. He looked back at her, confused as to why she was leaving in such a hurry, and without even saying good-bye. In her rush, she caught the heel of one of her crystal shoes on the palace steps. With no time to stop, Cinderella left it behind and took off. The prince found the slipper, picked it up, and held it to his heart. His princess had disappeared, a crystal shoe his only memory.

Cinderella made it home just in time. Her clothes were once again rags. Her carriage and beautiful white horses were gone. The footmen were nowhere to be seen. Her dream of being a princess was just that—a dream.

When the stepsisters came home from the ball, Cinderella asked if the princess had been there again tonight.

"Oh, yes!" said Darlene. "And she was more beautiful than last night."

"But something happened!" interrupted Della. "At the first stroke of midnight, the princess left the ball! All that she left was a crystal slipper. It broke the prince's heart to see her go."

"He doesn't even know her name!" added Darlene, jealously. "He will probably never see her again."

In the next days, the prince searched throughout the kingdom for the princess. Many a woman stepped forth and tried to convince the prince that she was the one he had danced with. But the prince knew better. The lovely face of the princess was etched into his memory. He could never mistake someone else for her.

In his last efforts to find the princess, the prince sent out an announcement.

> *Hear ye, hear ye,*
> *To all the fair ladies of the land*
> *Whom I met at my ball, so grand!*
> *I search for the one who stole my heart*
> *Whose beauty and loveliness set her apart.*
> *She left me with merely a slipper of glass*
> *And only the lady whose foot fits shall pass.*
> *If you are the princess who left me her shoe,*
> *I'll make you my wife, for our love is true!*

He sent out messengers searching for the right woman. If they found her, the prince would marry her without delay. This caused great excitement throughout the kingdom. Every woman prayed she would be the one whose foot fit into that fine crystal slipper.

The messengers went from house to house, trying to fit the tiny shoe onto women's feet. They found no perfect fit. At last, the men came to the house where Cinderella lived with her stepsisters and stepmother.

"We were at the ball!" the stepsisters exclaimed. "Try it on us!"

The messengers took out the tiny slipper and knew instantly it wouldn't fit either woman. But the sisters insisted, trying to squeeze their chubby toes into the shoe. The crystal slipper was just too small.

The men were about to leave when they heard a noise come from the back room. They stopped in their tracks.

"Is there anyone else here who should try on the shoe?" the messengers asked.

"No, no!" Cinderella's stepmother said with a laugh and a wave of her hand. "That noise was just our cinder-maid cleaning in the back room. There is no reason to try the shoe on her. She wasn't at the ball."

Cinderella, listening from the other room, stepped in to greet the messengers. She saw the slipper and asked to try it on.

Although she was covered in ash, the messengers found her beautiful and replied, "The prince said that every girl in the land shall be permitted to try on the shoe."

Cinderella sat down and pointed her slim foot. The messenger knelt down in front of her and put the crystal slipper on her. It fit perfectly. Cinderella smiled, thinking of her prince.

At that very moment, her fairy godmother appeared. With a wave of her wand, glitter and pink fog swirled around Cinderella. Within seconds she was once again the beautiful princess from the royal ball. The messengers declared on the spot that she was to be the prince's bride.

The prince was waiting on the palace steps when the messengers arrived with Cinderella. He walked slowly to the carriage. When the door opened and his eyes met Cinderella's, it was as if the ball had never ended. He took her in his arms and gracefully twirled her around, making sure she was real. Satisfied that the princess was once again his, he pulled her close and gave her a kiss.

Within days, Cinderella and the prince were planning a wedding. Their love was strong, and they were anxious to share their lives together forever. As for her stepsisters and stepmother, they would be left to do their own housekeeping and cooking, for their cinder-maid would be busy running a palace and living happily ever after with her prince.

CHAPTER 2

The Sleeping Beauty

ᏟᎣ

In an enchanted forest there lived a joyful couple: King Florestan and his wife, the queen. The couple owned lots of land, and had an exquisite castle and a large kingdom. What made the king and queen the happiest was their newborn daughter, Aurora.

The whole kingdom celebrated the birth of the couple's child. Flags were hung, bells rang throughout the land, and the king invited everyone to a christening feast. He also invited six little fairies to the party. Fairies lived in the kingdom at the time, and were expected to bring gifts to royal babies. There was one fairy, though, who was not invited. She was very angry the king and queen overlooked her.

Glorious skies greeted the christening day. People flocked to the palace. Many wonderful gifts were presented to the king and queen in honor of their baby daughter. They received precious jewels, silver spoons, and outfits made of lace and silk. But the most fantastic gifts of all were those given by the fairies. They performed a delightful dance around the cradle. The baby smiled as each one stopped before her and sprayed a mist of glitter over her cradle.

"Welcome, Aurora!" the first fairy said. "My gift to you is that you will always be beautiful! You will be the most beautiful woman in the world."

"And my gift," the second fairy said, "is that you will be as kind and charming as you are lovely."

The king smiled and bowed his head to the two fairies. He watched as the third fairy approached the cradle.

"I bring you the gift of wisdom. May you always know right from wrong and be able to make wise decisions." The little fairy floated away as the queen blew her a thank-you kiss.

The fourth fairy flew to Aurora with her arms outstretched. She kissed the baby softly.

"I bring you the gift of love, my child. You shall always love others and be loved by them."

The fifth fairy said, "I bring you song and laughter, little one. You will always be happy, and rarely feel blue." Humming a sweet tune, the fairy swirled around the cradle, acting silly to make the baby smile.

But when it was the sixth fairy's turn, the fairy who was not welcome at the party leaped into the cradle without warning. She threw sparks from her wand and gave the baby an evil look. She glared at the other guests who were gathered around the cradle.

"You thought I would go away, did you?" the ugly little fairy cried, staring at the king and the queen. "You thought you could take all these gifts and leave me out! Well, you are wrong, and I am here! I also have a gift. But Princess Aurora will not receive it until she is sixteen years old. Yes, all of the other fairies' gifts will arrive, but when the princess turns sixteen she will prick her finger on a spindle and die."

With an evil laugh and a forceful spin, the naughty fairy flew away. The king gasped at the fairy's words. The queen picked up baby Aurora and held her tightly, hoping to protect her. The good fairies formed a circle near the cradle and sadly watched the queen and her baby. The guests of the kingdom gathered together and cried.

The sixth good fairy, who had been inter-rupted before she could give her gift, fluttered over to the king, queen, and their baby. She said, "I know I cannot take away the wish that the evil fairy brought, but I *can* change it. Baby Aurora will not die from the finger prick. She will merely sleep until a chosen prince shall come and wake her with a kiss."

"She shall not die! She shall not die!" shouted the guests of the feast. Their smiles returned, and their voices were happy.

The king then put up his hand, asking for silence. "I want all spindles in the kingdom burned!" he cried. The people of the land happily obeyed, knowing it would keep their princess safe.

For years, life went on as planned. The fairies' gifts all came to be. Princess Aurora was the most beautiful, kind and charming, wise and loving young woman in the land. She was filled with the gifts of song and laughter. The evil fairy's gift was all but forgotten.

When the princess turned sixteen, she had a lovely birthday party. Many of the children from the town came to celebrate. They played for hours, but the princess tired of the games. She left her friends and went for a walk alone in the forest, a place she hadn't gone very often as a child. Aurora let her mind wander back to the wonderful party. She wasn't paying much attention to where she was walking. It was just getting dark when she realized she was lost. The princess noticed a small cottage ahead. She walked to the home and knocked on the door. At first no one seemed to be there. She peered in a window and saw an old woman who was twirling a stick between her hands. A long, soft blue thread spun through her fingers. She obviously had not heard the king's rule that all spindles were to be destroyed. The old woman noticed Aurora and motioned the young girl inside.

"What are you doing?" Aurora asked. She

had never seen anyone weave thread before and was very curious.

"I am spinning, my dear," said the woman.

"This is beautiful!" Aurora exclaimed as she touched the silken thread. "How do you do it? Can you teach me?"

Aurora had no sooner reached for the spindle than it pricked her hand. She fell to the ground.

The old woman quickly called for help. Aurora was brought back to the palace and placed on a bed of rose petals in the royal garden. The king and queen pleaded with the people of the kingdom for help. People from all over the land came to offer their services. They misted her with water, rubbed her with precious oils, and massaged her forehead. Nothing brought the princess out of the deep sleep she was in.

The people of the kingdom spent a few days trying to wake the princess. They talked about Aurora's accident so much that the sixth good fairy found out about it. She flew quickly to the princess's side and tried to awaken her. She was no more successful than the townsfolk. Rather than seeing the whole kingdom mourn for Aurora, she waved her wand and put everything around the girl to sleep. The birds stopped singing, and the beauty in the flowers faded. Even the king and the queen fell asleep in their thrones.

Around the palace and its gardens a hedge of thorny roses grew and grew until it covered the palace walls. It grew so high that the towers and the tops of trees could not be seen. Everything inside the palace was asleep, just like the princess.

The townspeople who were shut out of the palace were curious about what was happening inside. They tried their best to tear through the thorny bushes, but they could not. Occasionally, princes from faraway lands would come and try to fight through the hedges to get into the palace. They always found it too difficult and left with broken hearts. None of them knew why they were so strangely drawn to that place.

After a hundred years, another prince was riding through the land. This handsome gentleman was not out looking for a bride. He was on his way to a nearby city that needed help with important matters. He was very wise for his young age and respected throughout many kingdoms.

The prince was deep in thought as he passed the kingdom of the sleeping beauty. He almost didn't see the towers peeking through the jagged hedges. But a strange feeling tugged at his heart. He pulled out his sword and swung his weapon with all his might, cutting through the thick stems. It took much effort and many hours, but the prince finally broke through the jagged hedge of thorns.

He found the silence of the palace almost holy.

Nothing moved, nothing breathed. Everything was just as it had been left one hundred years ago. The prince gazed around him as he walked through the castle. His heart was mysteriously leading him to one place.

The prince walked to the royal garden, his heartbeat quickening with every step. It was there that he found her—the most beautiful woman he had ever seen. He hadn't even realized before that moment what he was looking for. Aurora was sleeping atop a bed of rose petals in the garden, just as she had been for a hundred years. Her cheeks matched the color of the flowers blooming all around her. Her hair was golden like the sun, and her lips were red as an apple.

The prince knelt before the princess and picked up her hand. He touched her face and gently tried to wake her, for he didn't know how she had come to fall asleep. If it weren't for her true loveliness, she may never have tasted life again. But the prince, his heart aching from her sad beauty, leaned down and kissed her.

The princess opened her eyes and gazed at the handsome man before her.

"My prince!" she cried. "I knew someday you would come! I have waited for so long!"

"How long have you been asleep?" the prince asked, still not sure why the princess had been left to lie in a garden alone.

"I listened to my parents discuss the story before they fell asleep, too," Aurora said. "Although I was not awake, I could still hear and understand everything that went on around me."

She told him the story of the fairies and the wonderful gifts they gave her when she was born. She also told him of the evil fairy who put her to sleep for so long. She explained how she had to wait for the right prince to save her.

"If only I had known before I touched the spindle . . ." the princess sighed.

"But then we never should have met," the prince said.

Aurora smiled back at the handsome man. "How did you know you were the prince chosen to find me?"

"This may sound foolish, but the need to be with you drew me near. My heart felt pure joy as I came down the road to your kingdom. How I was chosen, I do not know. All I know is that you are mine, and I am yours, if you will have me. We should spend our lives together, away from naughty fairies and old wooden spindles."

The princess nodded, her lips quivering. She was too happy to speak. As she hugged the prince, the rest of the palace came to life. Aurora's spell was officially broken! The birds began to sing again, the trees swayed in the summer breeze,

the people inside the walls of the palace awoke
and went back to their business of living. It was
as if time had never stopped.

Within minutes, the king and the queen
were at the princess's side. Seeing their daughter
awake and happy made them more joyful than
words could say.

"There shall be a wedding!" the king
announced, for it was plain to see that the
young couple had already fallen in love. Within
a week, the exquisite event took place.

All the people in the land were invited to
the celebration (except for one naughty fairy, of
course). The palace was draped in white and gold,
with candles lighting the steps and the entrance.
The pleasant scent of flowers filled the air.

This was a storybook setting for a wedding. Anyone could see the couple's future was
bright.

They were sure to live happily ever after.

CHAPTER 3

Coppélia

⁓

In a small village in the mountains there lived a toy maker named Coppélius. He mostly kept to himself, so the townspeople knew little about him. He lived in a great big house and spent much of his time working at making toys.

The townspeople also knew that Coppélius had a daughter. She was one more secret Coppélius kept to himself. Each night she would sit by her bedroom window and read. No one ever saw her leave the house. Occasionally, people would stroll by and wave at the beautiful woman in the window, but she never paid them attention. She sat still and focused on her book.

One summer evening, a villager named Franz walked by the toy maker's house. Glancing at the upstairs window, he saw the most beautiful woman he could ever have imagined. He stopped in his tracks and took a few moments to gather the courage to greet her.

"So, you see my daughter?" Coppélius said, suddenly appearing behind Franz.

"I do," Franz replied. "She is most lovely. What is her name?"

"Coppélia," the man said proudly.

"Her beautiful name suits her," Franz said, still gazing at the high window.

"It does indeed," Coppélius answered. "And what's your name, my boy?"

"My name is Franz, sir."

"Franz? What kind of a name is that?" the

man asked while he chuckled. Franz felt his face turn red.

"I'm just joking, my boy, just joking!" Coppélius laughed, knowing he had truly embarrassed the young man. "Franz is a fine name."

Franz didn't take his teasing so lightly. He forced a smile, only because he hoped to get invited inside to meet the man's daughter.

"You tricked me on that one, sir!" Franz said, trying to sound amused. He made sure Coppélius didn't know how rude he thought the man's comment was.

"I should be going now. It is time for my daughter to make me some tea."

Franz had a hopeful look in his eyes. Coppélius must have noticed. At once, the toy maker squashed any idea that Franz would be invited in for afternoon tea.

"It *is* sad that you can't join us, Franz. My daughter and I always take tea alone. It is our special time together to talk about the books she reads." Coppélius expected Franz to be disappointed.

"Perhaps another time?" Franz asked.

"Perhaps," Coppélius answered. "Or perhaps not!"

As rude as this old man was, Franz still could not give up hope that one day he would meet Coppélia. He held on to the image of her sitting in the window.

From that day forward, Franz made time to walk past the toy maker's house just to catch a glimpse of beautiful Coppélia. He would stand there, longing for her and looking up at the window, hoping she would see him. But every day was the same. The woman remained true to her reading, and Franz went home feeling rejected and hopeless.

There was another girl in Franz's life whom he was having a hard time forgetting. Swanilda was a kind and caring soul, but not an exquisite beauty like Coppélia. They had been friends for quite some time, and had recently talked of marriage. But Franz had put her off, wondering if he was indeed ready for that. Seeing Coppélia now every day made his situation even tougher.

Swanilda had heard of Coppélia and her unmatched beauty. She also learned of Franz's fascination with the toy maker's daughter and his daily walks to see the mysterious woman. It upset her to think of Franz's heart belonging to another. Swanilda decided she would soon pay a little visit to Coppélia and see what she thought of her Franz.

The very next night there was a celebration in the town to honor the hard work of the townspeople. Franz and his friends gathered in the streets, laughing and carrying on like a bunch of schoolboys. By chance, Coppélius walked by. He was wandering aimlessly through the town, singing to himself and not paying too much attention to where he was going. As he passed the group of boys, he tripped on a cobblestone. They laughed at foolish, strange Coppélius as he picked himself up.

"Coppélius, we meet again!" said Franz as he watched the man brush himself off.

"Yes, hello, my boy. You are the young man who has eyes for my daughter," Coppélius said.

"Is your daughter coming to the celebration tonight?" Franz asked, hopeful.

"No, Coppélia is not much for parties. She likes to stay in her room and read, as you know." The old man was having a little trouble standing up. He looked like he was in pain from his fall. He moved closer to lean on Franz. The young man had a bad feeling about Coppélius.

"I'm sorry, Coppélius, but I must go," Franz stuttered, moving away from the strange man. "Please give your daughter my best wishes."

Franz watched Coppélius wobble away, mumbling to himself.

After he was gone, Franz noticed a key on the ground. The young man grabbed it.

"I've got the key to his house!" Franz yelled in delight. His real pleasure was in possibly getting to meet Coppélia, but he enticed his friends with the fun of seeing the old man's toy workshop. On the way to the house, the young men met up with Swanilda and a few of her friends.

"Come along!" Franz spoke with excitement. "We've got the key to Coppélius's house."

Swanilda was happy to join in. This was a perfect opportunity for her to catch a glimpse of the mysterious young woman and hopefully talk to her. She giggled with the rest of the girls as they followed along toward the toy maker's house.

Franz opened the door with the key and motioned the boys in the house with him. They took off directly for the workshop. The girls were more nervous about entering the home. They cautiously stepped into the doorway. Swanilda was the only one who bravely pushed through, heading for the stairs to question the young woman. When she got to the upstairs room, she found Coppélia standing in the corner. Suddenly shy and nervous about breaking into the house, Swanilda felt like running for the door. But Coppélia didn't make even the slightest move. This seemed so strange that Swanilda went nearer to the girl.

"I want you to stop flirting with my Franz!" Swanilda said in a warning tone. "If you don't, you will have to deal with me!"

Coppélia didn't answer. Swanilda got very upset, thinking that the girl was ignoring her. She walked up to her and stood face-to-face with the beauty. She took her by the shoulder, meaning to get her attention. Instead, she found the woman stiff and cold. Swanilda couldn't believe it.

"Why, you are just a doll!" Swanilda gasped. She almost dropped to the floor in amazement. "How could we all have been fooled like this?"

Swanilda pushed the doll into the shadows. She grabbed the shawl from around the doll's shoulders and put it around her own shoulders. Suddenly she heard a commotion downstairs. It sounded like Coppélius had returned home and was forcing the boys and girls out of the house. Swanilda was frightened. She stood very still, expecting Coppélius to enter. Instead, she saw Franz appear in the doorway. Perhaps he was coming to save her!

The room was dark, and Franz tripped over some tools. Soon after, another person appeared in the doorway. Coppélius looked down and saw Franz slumped on the floor.

"I thought it was probably you in here, trying to see my daughter and rummage through my toys!" Coppélius said. He stepped behind the door and picked up a nearby broom to threaten Franz.

Franz stared back at the man. He didn't know what to say.

"I don't want you in here!" Coppélius said angrily. "Get out of my house!" He swung the broom right down on Franz's head. He was knocked out and, again, fell to the floor.

Swanilda wanted to run to Franz and see if he was badly hurt, but she had to keep control of herself if she was to quietly escape the house.

"Finally, I can now try my magic!" Coppélius exclaimed. "I will take the life from you, my sorry boy, and give it to my beautiful daughter-doll."

Coppélius had always wished his toys were alive. In his loneliness he had read many magic books and said many spells, hoping and wishing for real-life company. But he never even came close to bringing one of his dolls to life. Perhaps this would be the time.

The man leaned over Franz, who was still lying motionless on the floor. He mumbled a spell over his body. Then he shut his eyes and pointed to Swanilda. He thought she was Coppélia! He counted to ten then opened his eyes.

"Dance, my beautiful doll!" he said. "Please dance, my lovely Coppélia!"

Swanilda wanted to laugh out loud at the toy maker for thinking he could make such magic. But she also feared what he might do to Franz in his anger, so she went along with his demand. The young woman pretended the life of Franz had taken over her body. She spun around and began to dance mechanically, the way a doll would.

Coppélius nearly burst with excitement. "My magic has worked! My beautiful Coppélia has come to life! Hurray!"

Swanilda began to dance more gracefully around the room. She could spin around all night. But she feared she'd never be able to rescue Franz and escape from the toy workshop. As she twirled, her mind developed a clever plan.

Still acting like a dancing doll, Swanilda waltzed toward a shelf that held dishes. She picked up a saucer and threw it at the old man. Coppélius looked at her as if she was crazy.

Swanilda did another twirl and bent down to the floor to curtsy. There she grabbed a block of wood and flung it at Coppélius. She missed his head by inches.

"Stop it! Stop it, Coppélia! I am your father. Don't hurt me!"

The old man's words meant nothing to Swanilda. She thought of her poor Franz lying on the floor. It made her sad and angry. Coppélius had no more breathed life into a doll than she could make Franz fall in love with her. Swanilda began picking up more and more objects, throwing them left and right—a train set, a glass ornament, a puppet theater. She was nearly crazy.

"Please stop! You're hurting me!" he cried, trying to escape. "I must have done something wrong!" The old man ran around the room, dodging hammers, candles, and whatever else Swanilda could find to throw at him. Coppélius ran to the closet to hide.

At that moment, Franz opened his eyes. "Where am I? What happened?" Franz was now sitting up, rubbing his head. "Swanilda? Is that you?"

"Yes, my dear Franz, it is me," she said softly. "Let's get out of this place before the old toy maker returns."

"But—I don't understand," he said. "Where is Coppélia?"

Swanilda put her arm around him to

support his weight. They quickly left the house as Swanilda explained everything.

Franz looked up at the window from the spot where he had spent so long pining for his Coppélia. There he saw the old toy maker holding the life-size doll in his arms, crying onto her shoulder. Franz felt bad for a minute, but then remembered how Coppélius had tricked them all, pretending he had a daughter. No, this man didn't deserve sympathy.

Swanilda and Franz spent the next few hours together talking about their adventure. Franz thought Swanilda was brave to fool the toy maker. The more time they spent together, the more they fell in love. Within weeks, the couple was married in the village, where they celebrated with all their friends. The shy Franz and the bold Swanilda made a wonderful pair and lived a grand life together.

CHAPTER 4

Swan Lake

∾

Once upon a time, in the days of princes and peasants and castles, there lived a prince named Siegfried. He was an extremely handsome prince and very wise for his age. Prince Siegfried had just celebrated a birthday. It was an important birthday because the great prince was now of the age to be married.

"We shall have a grand ball in your honor, my son," his mother, the queen, announced. "You shall have your choice of any princess in the land."

For many princes, this would have been a dream come true. But for Siegfried, it was troubling. He was a kind and noble prince who had friends everywhere in the village. The peasant girls were every bit as beautiful and charming, if not more so, than any princess he had ever met. Why did he have to marry a princess?

The evening before the grand ball, Prince Siegfried left his friends at the castle gate and took a walk in the woods. He tried to be happy, but deep down he was miserable. He wanted to marry a lady for love, not because she was a princess. How he wished he would meet the perfect woman before tomorrow!

As the prince stopped to rest, a flock of swans flew overhead. They were flapping their way toward the setting sun, but circled at the last second to make a great landing on the pond.

The prince watched the beauties for a long time. In fact, it was the first stroke of midnight on the town's distant clock that brought him out of his long stare. As the prince gazed upon the pond, the swans swam one by one to the bank. When each bird reached the grass, it turned into a beautiful girl dressed in a costume of white feathers. The leader of the group wore a golden crown on her head.

"Dear prince," the leader said as she gracefully pranced toward him. "At last, you have come! I am Queen Odette and these are my maidens." The queen curtsied to the prince and smiled.

"We have had a spell cast on us by a wicked magician. We are human from midnight to dawn, but we change into swans when the morning comes. We remain in that form all day."

The prince simply stared at the queen, not knowing what to say. He had never heard a story so sad.

"The spell cannot be broken until I find a prince who will marry and love me forever."

The beautiful queen blushed after she spoke. Was it right to suggest to the prince he should love her? Little did she know that Prince Siegfried had fallen in love with her the moment he saw her.

And how could he help himself? Her eyes were a deep brown and her long, dark hair was swept up off her neck in a gorgeous swirl. Her

mouth was a lovely shade of red, and she had a childlike smile. She could warm any gentleman's heart.

As for Queen Odette, she had realized when she was dancing on the banks of the pond that Prince Siegfried was the only one for her. She had noticed him from afar when her flock of swans was landing. How handsome he was! He was tall and muscular, with light wavy hair and blue eyes. His gaze was intense, and his smile, upon seeing the queen, was welcoming and warm. To find a prince like him to break the spell would be too wonderful to imagine.

After the two looked into each other's eyes for a few moments, they began to dance.

The evening was perfect. The pond offered a symphony of summer sounds. The joyous rhythm of crickets chirping, frogs croaking, and nightingales singing was wonderful for dancing. The prince held the queen as if she were a flower that needed special care. They seemed to be so happy together. The other girls danced along with pleasure at the thought of their awful spell broken once and for all.

But as the couple began talking of their love for each other, a strange thing happened. A winged shadow crossed the pond. The atmosphere darkened. So did the queen's mood.

"Oh, no!" she cried.

"What is that?" asked the prince. A large owl swooped close.

"It is the magician in disguise—the magician who cast the spell on us!" Queen Odette cried. The owl flew just inches above her head. "He must know that you are the prince who has come to end the spell! I don't know what he will do to us."

The owl then swooped down close to the prince's head. Siegfried shouted so loudly at the attack that his friends overheard his cries and ran to help him. The group fought the owl unitl the owl flew away. The lovely ladies were safe again.

"You are truly my prince!" Odette said, smiling gratefully. "I don't know how to thank you!"

The queen gave the prince a hug and sat down beside him. She told him of the magician's evil. When the queen felt sure the owl was gone, and the mood was once again light, the group of ladies danced for Prince Siegfried and his friends. They thanked the men for their help and kindness. The prince then invited Odette and the ladies to the grand ball. They accepted the invitation and said they'd arrive around midnight.

As darkness turned to day, all the girls, including Queen Odette, turned back into swans. The prince returned to his palace, sad to see the queen leave. But he was happy knowing that she would be at the grand ball that night. Of course he would choose her as his bride. Once they were married, Queen Odette and her maidens could take off their feathers forever, because the magician's spell would be broken.

The grand ball was every girl's dream come true. There were guests from all over the world. Women wore gorgeous gowns with precious jewels sparkling in the light. They gossiped in little groups about their hopes of dancing with the prince. The gentlemen had all dressed in their finest, no matter how far they had journeyed. They gladly kept the ladies company as the women waited their turn to dance with the prince.

Just before twelve o'clock, a beautiful woman looking exactly like Queen Odette arrived at the palace. Prince Siegfried didn't notice it wasn't quite midnight yet. Upon seeing this beautiful girl, he sincerely thought she was Odette. However, the lovely lady who resembled the girl of Siegfried's dreams was not the true queen. In fact, she was Odile, the daughter of the wicked magician who had cast the swan spell. She was there to play a trick on him.

"I am so happy you have come," he whispered to her, guiding her across the ballroom. "You look lovely!"

Even though she was supposed to be mean to the prince, Odile was thrilled at his kind words. As the daughter of such a nasty man, she hadn't heard many nice things.

"I am so happy to be here," she responded.

"I know so little about you, my beautiful swan queen," the prince said, still captured by her beauty and her smile. "What can you tell me that will make me love you always?"

Odile blushed for a moment, her thoughts racing. Could she speak as well as Queen Odette would? "Why do you ask, my prince?" she asked, trying to avoid the question.

"I ask, my dear lady, because I want you to be my bride."

Odile knew she was only required to fool the prince for that one evening. After tonight, he would know she was not the real queen. He would never look at her again. Unless she could somehow figure out a way to make him love her!

She smiled back at the prince. "Of course I will marry you! I shall live to make you happy." Odile said these words with a glimmer in her eyes.

The prince turned Odile around slowly so the crowd could see her. He had never met anyone so beautiful. He would be so proud to call her his wife.

As Odile waved to the crowd, a loud clap of thunder suddenly shook the ballroom. The lights flashed and the chandelier swayed. The floor shook slightly. The guests in the ballroom began screaming in fear. What was happening?

At that very moment Prince Siegfried looked up and noticed the true swan queen at the castle window, tired and injured from beating her wings against the pane of glass. She had been trying to get his attention, but he had been entranced—by the wrong woman!

The prince looked from the window to the woman by his side and back again.

"I don't understand," he said. "How can there be two of you?"

In an instant, the woman by his side disappeared with a cloud of smoke. In her place appeared a short man. He was dressed in black and carried a wand.

"How do you feel now?" the magician asked, smiling wickedly at the prince. "You have just asked for my daughter's hand in marriage! Your pretty little swan queen never even made it through the door."

The evil man's plan had worked. Prince Siegfried had promised his love to a fake, not to Queen Odette. Now she and her maidens would remain swans the rest of their lives.

The prince was overcome with despair. He ran from the palace, knowing he must explain his awful mistake to his true love, Queen Odette. He found her weeping at the pond. She was in her human form since it was past midnight. Prince Siegfried, with tears of his own, took her in his arms and explained the magician's cruel plan. He asked for forgiveness. The generous woman forgave the prince and accepted her fate.

Queen Odette's heart filled with sadness. The more she thought of her future without the prince, the fuller her heart became. Within moments, Odette's heart was almost bursting. She could no longer live this life. There was no way she could exist without Prince Siegfried. Queen Odette buried her face in her hands and cried.

The magician came to the woods. He hoped to find the young lovers and boast about the trick he had played on them. As the magician approached, Prince Siegfried jumped from where he was sitting with Queen Odette to fight him. The prince was wild with anger at the evil little man. He kicked and punched him. The prince's very last blow threw the wicked man right into the pond. The heart of the magician was as black as coal and as heavy as a rock. The weight of it took him down, down, down to the bottom of the lake. He never surfaced again.

Odette's soft cries drew Siegfried's attention back to his love. Odette was dying from heartbreak. He ran to her side and took her hands in his. It was then that Siegfried decided that life without Odette would be unbearable. Looking into each other's eyes, they leaped into the lake and allowed the water to swallow them gently.

As the morning arrived, the maidens were filled with joy to find that they had not changed back into swans. Looking at the quiet beauty of the water, they saw a silhouette of the lovely

Odette and the man who loved her. The maidens knew the couple had broken the spell.

As for Prince Siegfried and Queen Odette's love—the lake, known forevermore as Swan Lake, was livened by the spirits of the couple every morning at dawn. As long as there is Swan Lake, there will be Queen Odette and Prince Siegfried—there in true love forever.

CHAPTER 5

The Little Mermaid

In the deepest part of the bluest ocean, there lived the Little Mermaid. Like all mermaids, she had no feet. Her body ended in a tail like a fish. Yet she was very beautiful. She was the daughter of a king, which made her a princess—an ocean princess.

As a young mermaid, the little princess dreamed of the time when she would be old enough to swim to the surface of the water. She had heard many wonderful stories about grand ships and brilliant city lights that could be seen there. When the mermaid turned fifteen, her father gave her permission to swim to the surface.

The Little Mermaid was delighted. She swam up that night. When she burst through the top of the ocean, she stared at the new sights.

The Little Mermaid found the perfect spot to watch big ships come her way. She waited for a few minutes then noticed a big white sail in the distance. The clouds were golden in the background, the Northern Star glittered in the sky, and the sea was as smooth as glass. She smiled at her good fortune.

The Little Mermaid swam closer to the ship to get a better look. She was able to see inside the cabin windows. There was a grand celebration going on. She saw a few older men chanting and singing. In the center of the action was a young prince. He could not have been more than sixteen. His eyes were large and dark, his hair wavy and light from the sun.

It seemed to be his birthday, which must have been the reason for the party. The men set off fireworks in honor of the prince. This burst of noise startled the Little Mermaid so much that she dove far underneath the water for some time before she felt it safe to return to the surface.

When she did, she saw the grand display of what looked like stars falling from the sky. She had never seen anything so beautiful. The burst of light made the area bright for a few seconds. It was just enough time for the mermaid to see the face of the handsome prince.

He was standing up on deck now, laughing and shaking hands with the others. She couldn't tear herself away from the sight of him. Soon, however, a change in the weather caused them all to move quickly. The waves began to roughen. A storm was close by. The men knotted the sails and took to their individual jobs. As the sailors tried to secure the ship, the storm began to wreck it.

The Little Mermaid almost laughed at first as she saw grown men panicking because of a little storm. Why, she had seen much, much worse in her short lifetime. But then she remembered that humans could not live in water, and she felt her heart quicken. She knew the prince was doing his best to save his shipmates.

The storm quickly demolished the ship. It was hard to believe that a short time ago it had been rocking gently and hosting a birthday party. Now it was gone. The Little Mermaid could see pieces of it scattered everywhere in the water. It was very dark. Even if any of the men had lived through the storm, they wouldn't be able to find one another.

The tearful mermaid could think only of the prince. Where was he? She could save him! Why wasn't he swimming to her? But of course, he didn't even know she existed. She needed to find him—and fast.

After a few tries, the Little Mermaid found the prince barely hanging on to a piece of wood. His eyes were already closing, but she could feel him looking right into her face. His strength was giving out, and if she had not found him just then, the prince, without question, would have died. She knew he wouldn't forget that a beautiful lady had come to his rescue.

The Little Mermaid swam to shore, pulling the prince along with her. She had hoped he would be awake by the time they reached the sand. Instead, he looked lifeless. His eyes were shut, and his cheeks were pale. She kissed his forehead and turned his face toward the sun that was now peeking through the clouds, hoping the warmth might wake him. Then she heard voices in the distance—human voices! She knew she'd have to hide. The Little Mermaid gave the prince one last look, then swam behind a nearby rock.

A group of nuns from a nearby church found the young prince on the shore. They picked him up gently and carried him away. The Little Mermaid had tears in her eyes. She had a feeling that when the prince awoke, he would not know exactly who had saved him from the storm. With an aching heart, she dove back under the water and swam as fast as she could to her home beneath the sea. She wanted to forget the prince, forget her trip to the surface, and live as a mermaid should—deep in the sea.

And so the Little Mermaid did for a while. Eventually, though, she missed her prince so much that she decided to tell her sisters about the boy she had fallen in love with. They might know what to do. Her dear sisters listened to her story.

"And I shall never see him again!" the Little Mermaid cried at the end of the tale. As her tears began to flow, she noticed one of her sisters smiling.

"I can find out where the prince lives!" the littlest sister announced. "I'll ask some of my friends to seek him out."

The Little Mermaid's sister spread the word about the prince. Sure enough, in very little time, the prince had been found.

"Come! We shall all go to the surface together!" the sister announced. "I know how to get to the prince's castle."

The Little Mermaid could barely believe her luck. After the first time she went to the prince's castle, she went there almost every evening. She swam up and down until she could see the prince, but he never saw her. She would have given anything to be with him, for even one day. She told her sisters about how much she wished to be a human.

"You know, there *is* one thing you can do if you truly want to become a real person," said another one of her sisters. "I wouldn't want to go there myself, but if you dare, you can go to the Witch of the Sea."

The Little Mermaid listened as her sister told her about the witch. It all sounded quite terrifying. Yet the hopeful mermaid had no choice but to go if she ever wanted a chance to be with the prince. Meeting the witch was scary, but the Little Mermaid was determined.

"I know what you want," the witch said before the Little Mermaid could even open her mouth. "Wanting to become a human is foolish, but I will grant your wish. You will lose your tail and have two legs grow in its place. Once the prince falls in love with you, you will become a human forever."

The Little Mermaid nearly tingled with delight. She wanted to shout about her love for the prince. But the witch held up her bony finger to stop the princess from speaking.

"I have a magic potion to give you that you

must take with you when you next swim to the prince's palace. You must sit on the shore and drink it. Once you have drunk the whole potion, the process will begin. I won't lie to you—it will hurt very much. It will feel like someone is cutting your body with a knife. But afterward, everyone who sees you will think you are the most beautiful woman they have ever seen. You will be graceful, but you will feel pain with every step. If you still want to go through with this, I will grant your request."

"Yes. Yes, I do." the Little Mermaid answered in a trembling voice. She could only think of the prince.

"But remember," said the witch, "you can never be a mermaid again. When you become a human, you can never go down to see your family or your home again. And if you don't win over the prince's love and become his wife, you will never have a full life. In fact, if the prince marries another, that very day your heart will break and you will die. You will change into foam and float on the waves of the sea."

"I still want to do this!" the Little Mermaid almost shouted. "Please do this for me!"

"Well, I do need payment, you know," the old witch said in a gruff tone.

"What do you want?" the girl asked, growing more impatient by the minute.

"You have the most charming voice of all the creatures of the sea. I know you would like to use it to attract your young prince, but your voice is something I must have."

"But if you take my voice from me," said the princess, "what do I have left to charm my prince?"

"You are so lovely," answered the witch. "The prince will fall in love with you before he even speaks to you. Listen, little one, I've used my own blood to make this potion. You know that I will take nothing less than your voice for payment."

"Fine!" the Little Mermaid said. "Take my voice. But go on! I want to find my prince."

"Here it is," the witch said, handing a bottle of liquid to the mermaid. At that same moment, she placed one of her bony hands on the mermaid's neck and the other hand on her own neck. The witch mumbled some magic—and that was it! She had captured the voice of the princess. Within seconds, the witch disappeared.

The Little Mermaid swam to the shore right outside the prince's palace. She sat on the sand, drank the potion, and . . . like a sword through her body, the pain began. When she could take no more, she lay back on the sand, lifeless and pale.

When the sun came up, she awoke. She was no longer a mermaid—she was human! The pain of her transformation was burning in every inch of her body. But standing before her was the man she had been waiting forever to meet again. The prince was looking at her, his dark eyes gazing into hers.

The Little Mermaid looked down and saw that her tail had indeed disappeared; two long, slender legs took its place. The young prince held out his hand and helped the girl to her feet. The pain that she felt when she stood was as horrible as the witch said it would be. As she and the prince walked toward the palace, she felt as if she were treading on sharp blades. But she took the pain, for being by the prince's side was worth it.

The prince asked her several questions as they walked—her name, where she came from, how she got here—but her voice was truly gone. She could only smile sweetly at the prince when he spoke.

When they arrived at the palace, the Little Mermaid was handed robes of silk. Everyone at

the palace agreed that she was the most exquisite beauty they had ever seen.

That afternoon, a girl of the court came to
sing for the prince and his parents. The Little
Mermaid felt her heart grow sad as she saw how
much everyone adored the singer. If only they
could hear her own voice!

And, the princess thought in silence, *if only he
knew that I gave up my voice for him.*

During the song, the prince took the Little
Mermaid's hand and began to dance with her. The
dainty girl twirled and cascaded across the room
so gracefully that she forgot about the guest with
the beautiful voice. Everyone was watching the
beautiful princess dance with the young prince.

It was decided that the Little Mermaid would
be a guest in the palace and have her own apart-
ment with the finest of things. She had riding
clothes made for her and went with the prince
on a horseback-riding trip. How strange this

was for her, riding on the back of a land animal for the first time! Quite often they got off their horses and walked until they were tired.

The Little Mermaid beamed throughout the day, she was so happy to be with the prince. But when the palace went to sleep that night, she walked out to the sea to place her feet in the water. She thought of her family and her far-away home. Although she was sad, she felt connected to them through the water. She decided she would visit the ocean every night.

The next night, while she was standing at the edge of the water, her sisters came swimming by, arm in arm. The Little Mermaid was so happy to see them! Her mermaid sisters sang a sad song to her. She motioned for them to come closer. She wanted to tell them how homesick she was, but also how happy she was to be with the prince. They couldn't get close enough to the shore to be near to her.

The mermaids came back to see their sister every night, even if they couldn't get close enough to talk. One time they brought their old grandmother with them. She had not been to the surface for many years. Their father, the Ocean King, also came to visit once. He had been angry and disappointed when his Little Mermaid left. But after his daughter had been away for so long, he began to forgive her. He longed to see her again. Their short visit reminded him of how much she had meant to him. A salty tear dropped from his face to the ocean.

Every day, the Little Mermaid grew dearer to the prince. He loved her like a sister, but he never thought of loving her as more than that. Yet, she *had* to become his wife so she could become a true human. Otherwise, as the witch had warned her, she would be changed into sea foam and forever toss over the sea.

One day the prince said to the Little Mermaid,

"You are more dear to me than anything else in the world. You remind me of a maiden whom I have been searching for. I was on board a ship that was wrecked in a sudden storm. The waves threw me on a shore near a temple. When I woke up, many maidens surrounded me. The youngest of them saved my life. I only saw her once, but I can still picture her face. She is the only one I will ever love. You look so much like her that I almost get confused. I have thought at times you may have been that maiden who saved my life. But I don't know how to find her again. I think fortune has granted me you instead."

How I wish I could tell him it was me who saved his life! the Little Mermaid thought with a sigh. *I carried him through that storm to the shore. I watched him from behind a rock as the maidens gathered around him, but I had brought him to safety.* She sighed deeply because she had lost her ability to cry when the witch captured her voice.

The prince readied his ship for a journey. "I must go and meet a beautiful princess," the young man said. "My parents say I must marry her," he added. "I will see her, but they cannot make me marry her! She cannot be as lovely as you. If I must choose to marry, of course I will take you, my silent girl with the speaking eyes." And he kissed her cheek and helped her get her own things ready to go along with him. The beautiful woman rarely left his side.

The next morning, the prince and the Little Mermaid sailed until they entered the harbor of the next kingdom. They arrived within a few hours and caught a glimpse of the beautiful princess whom the king and queen had chosen for their son. The Little Mermaid had a hard time accepting how perfect and lovely the woman's features were. Never had she seen anyone with skin so fair and eyes so dark and smiling.

"It's her!" the prince cried as soon as he laid

eyes on her. "She is the one who saved my life in the storm!"

No, it was me! the Little Mermaid wanted to cry. *I am the one who saved you!* But it was no use. The Little Mermaid looked at the prince, trying to pretend she was happy for him.

"I know, my sweet maiden, you will rejoice for me, because all you have ever wanted is my happiness," the prince said, looking into her eyes.

The Little Mermaid kissed his hand in her sorrow, thinking her heart would surely break. If his wedding day were soon approaching, then her death would also come soon.

The Little Mermaid took the prince's arm and tried to pull him back as he walked back to the princess.

"It is fine," he assured her as he escaped her grip. "I know now whom my heart belongs to. My parents have chosen wisely. This is my bride. Smile for me, for this will be my wedding day."

Bells rang and messengers hailed the news through the streets. The wedding took place that very afternoon. The Little Mermaid, dressed in silk and cloth of gold, stood behind the princess and held the train of her bridal dress. But the mermaid didn't hear the music, or see the beauty in the ceremony. She was losing the man she had given up everything for. She stared motionless at the happy couple in front of her. She could not believe this was happening. Her prince was leaving her. It was time for her to go, too.

The Little Mermaid disappeared from the crowd as soon as the prince and princess were married. She was sure no one would even notice that she was gone. All eyes were on the happy couple, and she would never be with him again.

The water looked inviting when the Little Mermaid reached the sandy beach. She walked along the sand for a moment, recalling the times she and her prince had played on the shore.

She now realized that the moments she had spent with the prince were truly wonderful, but selfish. It was time for him to be with someone who could speak and sing and share his life. A mermaid can never truly be a human. She is a treasure that is better to be kept secret in the deep blue sea.

A gentle breeze met her as the waves lapped over her toes. Her ankles moved through the salty water, and her feet took her deeper into the ocean. The water was past her knees and up to her waist. For a moment she looked out at the horizon and thought one last time about her prince. She felt her body slowly dissolving as she took her last steps into the water. She would now be nothing more than sea foam, the top of a wave forever trying to make it back onto shore.

Back at the wedding, the party moved to the

king's giant ship. All were celebrating the blessed day. The prince and his lovely bride held hands, looking out over the ocean.

"She's beautiful, isn't she?" the prince asked his new wife as they gazed out into the water.

"You mean the ocean?" the princess said, smiling.

The prince nodded. Just then, a cool ocean breeze sprayed a mist across the prince. It made him stand tall and look out into the horizon. It was almost as if someone had called his name. Familiar feelings of love and warmth spread throughout his body. And his heart beat like the heart of a man who had it all: the love of a princess and the secret treasures found only at the bottom of the sea.

CHAPTER 6

The Ugly Duckling

༷

It was a beautiful summer day. The wheat was golden, and the oats were still green. The hay was stacked in the lower meadow with the great woods and deep lakes behind it. In the sunniest spot stood an old mansion surrounded by a moat. There was a duck sitting on her nest in the leaves near the water. Her little ducklings were just about to be hatched, and she was tired of sitting. She had been there a very long time. Few visitors came around, so it seemed even longer.

Most ducks flying in would swim up and down the moat, not bothering to come into the weeds to see the mother.

At last one egg after another began to crack.

"Cheep, cheep!" they said upon being born. All the chicks had come to life and were poking their heads out. The tiny birds looked all around and then back to their mother.

"Quack! Quack!" she said, giving them something to practice.

"Quack!" repeated the ducklings happily.

"This is a big world, little ones," Mother Duck said. "It stretches a long way out from the other side of this garden. Let us go explore. Are you all here?"

Mother Duck counted quickly. "No! My biggest egg is still unhatched! How long is it going to take? I've been sitting on these eggs for so long." The mother duck sighed as she waddled back to the nest, lifted her body, and ruffled her feathers down on top of the one egg left. She looked a bit discouraged.

"I will sit on it a little bit longer. I've been here this long . . ."

At last, the egg cracked.

"Cheep, cheep!" said the young one as he tumbled out. How big and ugly he was! The other ducks looked at him.

"That is a huge duckling!" said the mother. "None of the others looks like that. I wonder if he's a turkey chick that got mixed up with my eggs. If he can swim, he's definitely a duckling. If not, well, then who knows? He will go in the water, even if I have to force him in myself. All right, my darlings! Let's all go to the water!"

Splash into the water the mother duck jumped. "Quack!" she said.

One little duckling dove in behind her. He went under the water but popped right back up. Another duckling jumped in. He came up and floated

beautifully. Before long, every duck was swimming, even the big ugly gray one they had doubted.

"He can't be a turkey!" said the mother duck, feeling sorry for the poor baby. "See how nicely he uses his legs and how straight he holds himself. He is my own chick! He is not so ugly and slow when you see him up close."

The ugly little duckling followed his mother, as did all the other ducklings, into the duck yard.

"This is where we will be spending a lot of our time, my darlings," Mother Duck explained. "There is plenty of water in the duck pond for us to play and swim in. The farmer also brings our food here. You must learn to get along with the other ducks, but be ready to defend yourselves, too."

There were two groups of ducks fighting over some food, and some quacking was going on in another part of the yard.

"Remember to quack correctly, and bend your neck to the old duck over there. She is the grandest one of all! She has a red rag around her leg. No one, not man or animal, is to cross her.

"Follow me!" the mother said, leading her crew proudly. "Quack now! Don't turn your toes in! Keep your legs wide apart! That's it! Now bend your necks and quack!"

The ducklings did as they were told, but the other ducks in the yard laughed at them. "Look there—as if there weren't too many of us here already! And look at that ugly duckling! We won't stand for him." A nasty duck flew by and bit the ugly duckling on the neck.

"Let him be!" the mother said. "He is doing no harm!"

"Maybe not," the biter said, "but he is so ugly, it doesn't matter. He needs to be taught a lesson."

"You have other children who are quite handsome," said the old duck with the red rag around her leg. "It's a pity you can't make this one over again."

"He may not be handsome," said Mother Duck, "but he has a kind heart and swims as beautifully as any of the others. I believe he will be very strong and find his way in the world."

The mother duck looked tired from teaching her little ones all morning. Taking care to protect the gray one was especially tough.

"Well, you and your ducklings may stay in the duck yard," the old duck said, feeling some pity. "Just try to stay out of my way."

Mother Duck and her little ones settled in. The first day passed without any problems, but each day afterward things grew worse and worse for the ugly duckling. The poor thing was chased and teased by everyone, even his own brothers and sisters. They told him, "We wish the cat would get you, you ugly thing!" The ducks bit him, the hens pecked him, and the girl who fed the ducks kicked him aside.

His mother could barely stand it anymore. She told him, "I must send you miles away from here. It's the only way I can think to protect you." She gave him strict directions to his uncle's pond and told him not to stray. She kissed him good-bye and promised she would see him again soon.

The ugly duckling took off right over the

hedge that divided the duck yard from the rest of the pond. Little birds flew up into the air in fright.

They flew away because I am so ugly, thought the poor duckling, shutting his eyes. He blinked away some tears and continued to travel on. Eventually he came to a swampy land where wild ducks lived. He was so tired and miserable that he decided to rest there the whole night.

In the morning, some wild ducks flew up to see the visitor.

"What kind of creature are you?" they asked as the duckling floated in the water. "You are very ugly. Where did you come from?"

The ugly duckling let out a sigh and turned away. He didn't want to talk to these mean creatures. He just wanted to lie among the leaves and drink some marsh water. Soon the wild ducks flew angrily away. Once he was alone again, he stayed in the marsh for two whole days without anyone bothering him.

Then two wild geese came. "Hello. You are a different duck. Where did you come from?"

The ugly duckling put his head down in shame. "I live nearby," he lied. "I am here for a walk."

The two geese had no reason not to believe his story. "Would you like to come with us to another marsh nearby? There are some charming wild geese there."

At that moment, the ugly duckling heard a *bang!* from the distance. Both the wild geese dove among the leaves and disappeared. Whole flocks of wild geese flew up from the tall grass as the loud noise rang out again. The duckling was confused. What had happened? Where had everyone gone?

The ugly duckling was scared. He sensed danger, so he hid within the tall grass and waited. It wasn't until the end of the day that he felt safe to leave the marsh. When he did go, he flew across fields and meadows, fighting the wind. He found it hard to make his way.

The ugly duckling knew he couldn't go back to where he had come from. He wasn't liked there. Instead, he explored new places, hoping to find a happy home somewhere. He came upon a small stream not too far down the road from a little cottage. It was empty of ducks and geese.

Taking a great running leap off the bank, the ugly duckling landed in the water. It felt wonderful! He floated along the top then bobbed up and down, splashing everywhere. He had a few hours to himself to feel the joy of being in the water once again.

But as he'd expected, other creatures soon came to the pond. They made fun of the ugly duckling when they arrived. It seemed this lovely place wasn't right for him, either.

The autumn was coming. The leaves were turning colors, and the wind was making them dance. The sky looked cold and the clouds were heavy. The poor little duckling didn't know what to do. He had seen other birds gather in flocks and fly high overhead together. Was that what he was supposed to do? His mother hadn't had a chance to teach him these things before he left home.

The ugly duckling was cold and uncomfortable. He tried snuggling in some bushes to keep warm. Nothing worked. He was still miserable, cold, and—what he hated most—lonely.

One evening, as the duckling paced back and forth, a flock of grand birds arrived. The duckling had never seen anything so beautiful. The birds were pearly white with long, slender necks. They swam elegantly on the water and made soft calls that were graceful and lovely. The duckling watched them for a minute. He was filled with disappointment as they spread their wings and flew away to warmer lands.

The duckling was overcome by a strange

feeling. He wanted to follow them, but he knew he'd never be able to keep up with the stunning creatures. When they were out of sight, he dove down into the water, touched the bottom with his beak, and came to the top again. He was still trembling with the strange feeling. He didn't know what the birds were, or where they had flown, or why he felt the need to see them again. He never felt more ugly than at that moment.

The winter came fast, and the ugly duckling thought he'd found a secure place to live through the season. Maybe the graceful birds would eventually return, he thought. It was so cold that he had to swim the pond in circles every day to keep it from freezing. Every night, the hole in which he swam got smaller and smaller. At last he was so weary that he could move no more. The poor duckling had frozen into the ice.

Early the next morning, a poor old man came along and found the frozen duckling. He walked out to the duckling and broke the ice around him. He then carried the poor thing home. The man's wife gave him food and warmed him up. But the man's three children were not so kind. The boys wanted to play with the duckling, but they were rough. They pulled his tail and poked his neck. They chased him through the house and onto the counters, where he spilled milk and knocked over the flour. The man's wife shrieked, but the old man just laughed. When the oldest child opened the door, the duckling flew outside, for that was his only chance to escape the craziness. He flew into the bushes and the newly fallen snow. There he rested and tried to catch his breath while recovering from the horrors of that house.

There were other bad things that happened to the ugly duckling during that winter, but it would be too sad to tell them all. Through the harsh season, he continued the search for food, warmth, and love.

But eventually, the sun made the earth warm again, the larks began to sing, the marsh became green again, and the ugly duckling welcomed the spring with joy. At least he'd now have the beautiful earth for company, if not other birds.

The ugly duckling spread his wings, surprised at the strength he felt in them after that brutal winter. He lifted himself high in the air and looked down upon the scene below. He saw a large garden where the apple trees were in full bloom and the air smelled like lilacs. Where the apple trees stopped, a beautiful lake began.

In that lake he saw three brilliant white birds—the same birds he had seen before winter arrived! He had been thinking about them all through the cold months. They were swimming toward him, their feathers barely touching the top of the water.

If I go down to them, they will peck at me because I am so ugly, the duckling said to himself. *But that doesn't matter. I would rather risk it all to meet those lovely birds. I must find out what they are!*

So the ugly duckling flew down to the edge of the lake where the swans were bathing. They saw him and moved over to where he was, their feathers ruffled.

"Make fun of me! Go ahead, peck at me!" said the poor creature, bowing his head toward the water. He shut his eyes tight and waited for the pain. But he felt none. The duckling slowly opened his eyes and was startled beyond words.

He saw his own reflection in the lake's glassy water staring back at him. But he did not see a dark gray bird, ugly and clumsy. He was a swan! He must have accidentally been born into a family of regular ducks. He finally knew who he was and where he belonged. The other swans invited him into the lake, and he joined them proudly. The big swans swam around him and stroked him with their bills. For the first time, the ugly duckling had a real family.

Some little children came with bread and corn to throw into the lake for the swans to eat.

"There is a new swan!" one of the children cried. "A new one has come!" They clapped their hands and danced around, making up songs about the new bird.

"He is the most beautiful one by far!" one of the girls said. The other children all agreed.

The little swan felt very shy. He hid his head

beneath his wing, unsure of how to take these kind words. But he was so happy! He promised himself he would never forget how things once were. He would never forget how he was teased and abused, and how he spent many months alone, friendless and without family.

He ruffled his feathers joyfully and raised his slender neck with pride. His heart sang, "I never dreamed of so much happiness when I was the ugly duckling!"

CHAPTER 7

The Firebird

୍ଠ

There once was a deep, dark forest. It wasn't a spooky one, but it was just strange enough that no one from the kingdom chose to live there. The ground of the dark forest was rarely ever walked upon. In fact, even the animals of the forest—rabbits, foxes, deer, squirrels—chose to make their homes elsewhere.

Sunshine rarely made it through the thick trees. Few flowers bloomed. Occasionally, a hearty daisy might peek her head through the shrubs. Sometimes a wildflower would come out. But for the most part, the woods were empty of earth's colorful life.

However, there was a tree in that forest. It was a very special tree that followed none of the forest's rules. This tree was average in height and size, but there were other things about it that made it special.

Its leaves were spectacular. They had such a variety of colors, and not just the usual autumn ones. These leaves glistened. Each one sparkled as if it had been polished. The shapes of the leaves were just as unusual as the colors. Some leaves looked like those of a maple tree, a few resembled oak leaves, and others looked like they came from a birch tree.

But the strangest and most wonderful thing on the tree was its fruit. It didn't bear just one type. There were apples, oranges, pears, and plums, to name only a few. The branches bent over with all the tasty choices.

The tree was a mystery to anyone who heard about it. Few actually saw it, of course. But those daring people who visited the forest found it incredible.

One day, there was a strange flutter in the woods that had never been heard before. The unusual sound grew louder and louder. It was like a low thunder. Suddenly, a great golden bird flashed like lightning through the leaves of the unusual tree.

It was a bird that looked as if it were made of fire. Its feathers were bright red and orange. Its eyes were like hot, glowing marbles. The tail of the bird was like a shooting star in the night sky. A more beautiful sight would be hard to find.

On the outskirts of the forest, there lived a prince. Prince Ivan was a kind and handsome man. Occasionally he walked the forest paths, which reassured the people in the kingdom of his bravery.

On the night of the firebird's arrival, Prince Ivan happened to be taking one of his walks through the forest. He saw the spectacular bird flash through the trees and settle on a low branch. He figured it would be a great prize to take it home and show his kingdom. He hid in the bushes and within minutes, the bird swooped down, and Prince Ivan caught him in his arms. The bird struggled, but the prince held on tight. Then something very strange happened. The large creature began to talk.

"Let me go!" said the firebird. "Let me go and I will give you something wonderful."

"What can you give me that could possibly be so special that I would let you go?" the prince asked. "Every man, woman, and child in my kingdom would like to see a fine creature like you."

"What if I gave you this?" said the firebird, plucking a golden feather from his breast.

"It is a beautiful feather," said the prince, "but how can it possibly do anything for me? It is just a feather."

"I promise it will someday prove special to you. Perhaps it will even save your life," the firebird said.

The prince laughed at the thought of a feather actually doing such a thing. "But it *is* too lovely to turn down," he added. "I will take the feather, and you can keep your freedom."

The firebird heard these words and flew off. The prince was about to leave, too, when he heard a sweet song sweep through the forest.

It took the prince a few minutes before he could actually find where the music was coming from. Finally he spied twelve lovely maidens singing the melody.

The girls were dressed in long, white gowns. They wore wreaths of pink and white flowers upon their heads. The most beautiful things about them were their voices. They sang as sweetly as angels. Never had the prince heard anything like it. He sat down, gazing at them. They seemed perfect in every way.

The lovely group of women created a circle around the mysterious tree. There they were joined by a lovely princess. She wore a white-and-gold robe, which hung loosely over her shoulders. They all took turns shaking the tree and catching the falling fruit—golden pears, silver peaches, and ruby apples. They threw one to Prince Ivan and he took a bite.

The prince was delighted by the company and the delicious fruit. He stopped chewing and introduced himself to the princess. The lovely princess curtsied, but then told the prince she was quite scared for him. This was odd because the princess herself didn't seem frightened at all.

"Don't stay here," she warned him. "This is a dangerous place—look!"

Glancing over to where the princess was pointing, the prince saw the walls of a large gray building. Although it was almost completely hidden by trees, it wasn't far away.

"That," the beautiful princess said, "is the castle of Kastchei."

"And who exactly is Kastchei?" asked the prince.

"Haven't you ever heard of him?" the princess asked in disbelief. "He is . . . a monster, I guess I should say. He sometimes looks human, sometimes animal, but most of the time he looks like a demon. He will do terrible things to any man he finds on his land. And we are on Kastchei's land."

"That doesn't bother me," said the prince. "I will stay here."

No sooner were the words out of Prince Ivan's mouth than there was a crashing sound. As if by magic, the girls disappeared. The trees began to shake, the earth quaked, and everything went black. The prince tried to find an escape path in the darkness, but he could find no way out.

In a blaze of light, a crowd of dark, devilish monsters appeared. The creatures had strange faces. Their mouths were shaped like circles, and their low, growling voices came out as a great howl. Their eyes, tiny and green, seemed to glow like candles. They had long, bony fingers with jagged claws. And the prince was surrounded by them!

He had nowhere to run or hide. In a matter of seconds the group grabbed him. He struggled to get free, but he found it impossible.

Then in a crash of thunder and a flash of lightning, the most horrible of the monsters appeared. He was terrible to look at! He had the shape of a man, but wiry black fur covered his entire body. He resembled the rest of the monsters, but he appeared to be much stronger.

He looked meaner than the others, if that was possible.

"Are you Kastchei?" the prince asked, not actually expecting an answer. The monster growled. The princess had not lied. He certainly was a terrible demon.

"Why are you here, in my forest?" the creature barked, surprising Prince Ivan with a human voice.

The prince's mind was racing, searching for answers. The demons were so much bigger than he was. He would never stand a chance in a fight.

"Why are you here?" the demon growled again, seeming even angrier than before.

"I don't know," the prince said honestly. He was looking at the group, still trying to find a way to escape.

"It is no use trying to get free," the beast said. "No one who enters my land may ever leave it. When I cast my spell over you, you will become one of my devilish crowd."

Kastchei raised his hand as if to hit the prince. But the prince remembered the firebird's life-saving feather. He quickly pulled it from his jacket and waved it in front of Kastchei. In an instant the glorious firebird appeared. The creature looked like a ball of fire as he swooped down.

The monsters forgot about the prince while they watched the brilliant bird. They became almost powerless in his presence. Kastchei also stood very still, shaking with fear.

The firebird looked to the prince and flew close to him, whispering, "Go to the bottom of the tree that bears the many fruits. There is a hole there. Crawl into it and bring out what you find. Hurry, while I distract the demons!"

The prince ran to the tree, tempted to continue down the path and all the way out of the forest. But the firebird had seemed sure of what he was asking. The prince decided it best to follow the bird's request.

Quickly Prince Ivan returned with an iron box. Kastchei was still in the same spot, his hands trembling.

"Open the lid," said the firebird.

Prince Ivan did as he was told. Inside was an enormous egg, which the prince took out of the box.

"This is the reason why Kastchei is shaking with fear," said the firebird, holding up the egg to show the prince as he began to tell this story:

"Many years ago, a princess lived in a cottage in this forest. More than anything else in the world, she loved to sing. She invited a group of twelve lovely maidens to live with her. Together they sang beautiful songs under the apple tree by the cottage. They always sang for the birds and other animals.

"One day, Kastchei—the evil one here—came upon the women. Trying to impress the ladies, he began to sing, too. He began howling, his voice quite sour compared with the maidens' voices. The women laughed at him and covered their ears.

"Kastchei became so angry that he began to throw apples from the tree at the maidens. As he threw them, the strangest thing happened. The apples turned into different types of fruit. And not just types of fruit to eat. They also turned into peaches sparkling with ruby dust and plums with crystal dew. The maidens were overjoyed.

"Of course, Kastchei didn't want them to be happy. He was so mad that he climbed up onto the higher branches of the tree. There, he saw me sitting in my nest."

The prince was so involved in the story that he did not notice Kastchei standing behind him.

THE FIREBIRD

The magician took a few steps toward Prince Ivan. The darkness of the forest was hiding him well.

"What happened then?" the prince asked.

"He saw what a beautiful bird I was, and he tried to capture me, just as you did. But I was ready for him. I flew quickly from my nest. When I did, he grabbed my egg, jumped down from the tree, and started to run."

"And then?" asked the prince, still unaware of the demon moving closer to him.

"Aside from being a wonderful singer, the princess was also magical. She performed a spell that captured the spirit of Kastchei and put it into the egg. And his spirit has been there ever since. To get rid of Kastchei, we would need to—

"Look out!" the firebird shouted suddenly. He'd noticed that Kastchei was about to attack the prince.

Kastchei jumped at the prince, trying to take the egg before it could be destroyed. But he was too late. The prince threw it to the ground. The egg smashed into pieces and, as a piercing scream filled the air, everything went completely dark.

When the light finally returned in the morning, everything had changed. Kastchei was gone. Even his castle had disappeared. The mob of monsters was now a group of handsome young men and lovely girls who had all been under his spell. The beautiful princess returned with her twelve maidens just as magically as they had disappeared. The maidens carried a crown and royal robe for their lovely princess, and they knelt when they stopped before Prince Ivan. They thanked him for his bravery.

The princess explained that they had to escape when Kastchei appeared because they feared for their lives. He would have destroyed them. But the princess knew in her heart that Prince Ivan could defeat the evil one.

"I am sorry we abandoned you in his presence," the princess said quietly.

"Do not worry about that now. Think of this instead: Will you be my lady?" the prince asked, drawing the princess close to him.

"Yes," said the princess. The crowd cheered.

It seemed the maidens and noblemen were not the only ones happy to see the royal couple together. At the moment the two were united, a burst of fireworks lit up the skies—sparkles of red, orange, blue, and green rained down over them.

Some say it was the spirit of Kastchei, broken forever, sprinkling light down upon the dark forest. But the prince, looking skyward at the fireworks, thought for sure he saw a bird, once made of fire, fading into the bright orange sunset.

CHAPTER 8

The Nutcracker

ᴄᴏ

The night was magical. Christmas Eve always was for Clara Stahlbaum. In her short seven years on earth, the brown-eyed little beauty loved no holiday better. The house was filled with merriment and good cheer. Holly sprigs hung from the curtains, candles burned in every room, and freshly cut pine wreaths greeted visitors at the door. And in the drawing room . . . well, that had to be left to Clara's imagination. Her parents were hosting a party in there, and she and her brother were not permitted to go in until after the grown-ups had left for the night.

"Can you see anything?" Clara whispered to her brother, Fritz, his nose pressed up to the keyhole of the drawing room door.

"Just a lot of people dancing," the younger one said with disappointment. "I don't think they're ever going to leave."

Clara's sigh matched her brother's. He was two years younger, and she suspected that he was having an even harder time waiting for the party to be over. He was still new to Christmas Eves and wasn't sure what to expect. He had just heard magical holiday stories from his older sister.

"Clara, are you sure there will be gifts for us tonight?" Fritz asked, his eyes wide with excitement.

"Oh, yes!" Clara answered quickly. "God-papa Drosselmeir would never come here on Christmas Eve without presents for us!"

Fritz smiled with relief and put his eye back up to the keyhole, hoping the dancing people might have magically disappeared. Clara watched him stretch his neck to get comfortable. The little girl sat down at the table and made a list of the presents she hoped to get this Christmas.

"They've turned down the lights!" little Fritz suddenly shouted, finding it hard to believe the time had finally arrived. "I can see the tree! I can see the tree!"

Clara gave her brother a slight nudge, allowing her to look through the keyhole. Fritz was right. The candles on the tree were lit, and the dance floor lights were dimmed.

Clara clapped her hands with joy when she heard her mother's footsteps near the door. She and Fritz pulled back and waited for the latch to turn.

"Oh, Mother! Is it really time?" Clara asked,

throwing her arms around her mother's waist. "Can we come into the drawing room now?"

Little Fritz did not wait for an answer. He flew past her through the door.

"Wait for me!" Clara called, praying no one would stop them.

The two children ran past the last few party guests and right to the tree. Dozens of tiny candles twinkled there like stars. All the toys underneath the tree and ornaments hanging from its branches glittered like treasure.

"Oh, it's beautiful!" Fritz whispered. It must truly have been one of the most wonderful sights of his life. Even with all the gifts around, he didn't take his eyes off the towering tree.

Clara, on the other hand, trembled in delight as she eyed the gifts. She giggled and clapped her hands and buzzed all around the tree, her eyes taking in all that they could. She finally decided to stop in front of a large gold box. There was a

wide bow tied on top and a little card that read CLARA. She carefully pulled it away from the tree and gave it a little shake. Taking no time to guess, Clara tore the wrapping and opened the box.

"She's lovely!" Clara exclaimed as she reached in to find a large, porcelain doll with features similar to her own. The straight hair and dark eyes looked as cute on the doll as on Clara. "She's beautiful, Mama. I shall call her Miss Claire."

By this point, Fritz had pulled his eyes away from the tree and spotted a tiny army of toy soldiers mounted on white horses. He let out a holler and pounced on the troops like a cat on a mouse. The men in the room smiled as Fritz played. He made a shrill sound as he knocked soldiers down from still horses.

Clara continued, opening gift after gift until she had opened them all. She sat on the floor, Miss Claire in one arm and, in the other, a silk dress with a ribbon on the front. Her mother and she watched as Fritz opened the last of his gifts— a set of new riding pants for when the new mare came. Clara didn't know which her brother was more excited about: Christmas Eve or a new horse coming to the barn. After watching him tear through the presents with glee, she was certain it was Christmas.

The evening was perfect. Clara thought it couldn't possibly get better when Godpapa Drosselmeir approached them at the tree. He had brought along his nephew, a shy young boy.

"And how have we done here, children?" Godpapa Drosselmeir asked, kneeling down beside them.

"Godpapa!" Clara shouted, wrapping her small arms as far around his neck as she could. She gave him a squeeze and a big kiss, happier than if she had seen Santa Claus himself.

He was a rather large man with a snow-white

beard and snow-white hair. He wore little glasses when he read, and always wore a jacket and tie. Clara's favorite thing about him was his smile. It wasn't that it was so unique, but it was always there. Their godpapa found pleasure in everything.

The children had always liked him, reaching their tiny hands out to him even as infants. This time was no different.

"Do you have more presents?" Fritz asked, still staring in disbelief at all his new treasures.

"Fritz! You don't ask like that!" Clara exclaimed, a little embarrassed. Fritz was such a young boy, though, and didn't know better.

The gentleman patted the small boy's head and stood up. He smiled and pretended he had to think about his answer. Clara could tell this was a sign that he did indeed have something else for them. He stepped back and stretched far behind the tree. With one hard pull, he presented a large flat box. It was decorated with a fancy red ribbon. The box was so large that it now took up most of the room in front of the tree.

"Open it!" Godpapa Drosselmeir said to the two children.

Clara had never seen a package quite so big. The only thing she imagined could be bigger was the mare coming to the barn. But that couldn't possibly be put in a box and kept behind the Christmas tree!

Fritz was working on removing the lid way before Clara even came close to untying the ribbon. When the lid was loose enough, the children each grabbed a side and carefully lifted it. When they looked inside the box, Clara and Fritz both let out squeals of delight. There was a shiny golden palace with pointed towers and rows of windows. Godpapa Drosselmeir then turned a brass key in a keyhole at the bottom, and the beautiful castle suddenly came to life. Soldier figurines marched out of the palace and paraded in four straight rows. Delicate women in exquisite hats and men in their best suits strolled past the castle windows. There was dancing in the miniature courtyard and a jester on the lawn. A beautiful princess waved from the balcony, trying to get the attention of a prince who was talking to the king and queen. A lovelier scene couldn't have been imagined.

The children sat, staring in fascination for several minutes. It was finally Fritz who broke the silence after seeing the figures complete their routines several times.

"I'm going back to my soldiers, Godpapa!" the little boy said with a smile. "Thank you for the gift. I will watch it more later."

Godpapa Drosselmeir gave the boy a nod and watched him sit down with his army. Clara was still interested in the palace, and didn't mind sitting for a while longer. She also didn't want to hurt her godpapa's feelings and leave the playland too soon. As she sat watching the tiny villagers, she noticed something else hiding far beneath the tree. It was bright red. She thought of asking Fritz to slide under and get it for her, but then thought better of it. She didn't want to take him away from his fun.

Clara ducked under the lowest branches, using her fingertips to slide the object toward her. When she finally got out from under the tree, she saw that she had pulled out a little man made out of wood. He had a strange look to him. He was almost like a soldier, but he had very short legs and an oversize head. He was wearing a green cap and a black cape on his back. He had black leather boots and shiny brass buttons on his coat.

Clara had never seen anything like it. She picked it up and held it carefully in her hands.

She studied his face, deciding that he had a kind look about him. His eyes were green. His delicate red lips seemed strange on such a military man. There was something different about him that made Clara simply fall in love.

"Oh, Godpapa!" she whispered. "He is beautiful. Who is this gift for?"

Godpapa Drosselmeir smiled. Rather than answer her, he picked up a nut, put it into the wooden soldier's mouth, and pulled the wooden cape down. He watched the little girl's eyes light up when a nut came out, ready for eating. He was amused by her interest in such an everyday tool.

Clara clapped her hands, never having expected such a trick. She jumped up and down with delight.

"I do believe this little nutcracker belongs to you," Godpapa Drosselmeir said with pleasure. "But I expect you to share it with your brother."

Clara would have traded both Miss Claire

and her silk dress for the nutcracker. Sharing it with Fritz would be no problem. He didn't even like nuts.

"He's ugly!" Fritz said when he finally stopped playing with his soldiers long enough to see Clara's new gift. But Fritz, not wanting to miss his turn at anything, tried to stuff the mouth of the nutcracker with nuts. Clara tried to stop him.

"You'll break him!" she said, trying to grab it from her brother.

Fritz held on tight and clamped the cape down hard. The nuts tumbled to the floor, along with three teeth from the nutcracker's mouth. The poor soldier's jaw was now crooked and wobbled loosely when Clara took it back.

"You've broken him!" the little girl cried. Cradling the nutcracker to her chest, she ran from the room, tears spilling down her cheeks.

Seconds later, Mother entered the drawing room. She said that the night had been long and that good boys and girls should go to bed. Clara saw her godpapa and his nephew getting ready to leave. She ran to the door to hug him good night. She thanked him for the toy palace and, most importantly, for the nutcracker. Fritz thanked him, too. Mother almost had convinced Fritz to go straight to his bedroom, but he stopped one last time to play with his soldiers and horses.

As Mother carried the pouting Fritz to bed, Clara sat under the tree and looked at the nutcracker. While she was thanking Godpapa Drosselmeir, Fritz must have tried to put the teeth back into the nutcracker's mouth. They were placed in the right spots, but crooked, then wrapped with a ribbon from a package. It was such a sweet attempt at a repair by her little brother. She would have to remember to thank him in the morning. But for now, she just wanted to hold her nutcracker and wait for Mother under the tree.

Clara held him for only a short time before

she began to feel sleepy. She surely couldn't have shut her eyes for more than a second. But when she opened them, the nutcracker was in a different spot.

"He couldn't have moved by himself," the little girl whispered, moving to where the wooden toy had gone. Just holding him reminded her of the fun she'd had earlier. She pulled the nutcracker toward her, gave him a hug, and left the drawing room for her bedroom. She put Miss Claire into the doll crib by her bedside. She fit nicely. Clara gave her a kiss and was just about to jump into her own bed when she heard the grandfather clock in the drawing room begin to chime.

Clara snuck out her bedroom door and glanced down the hall, expecting to see the wooden owl that was perched on top of the tall, thin clock. Instead, she saw the strangest sight. There, sitting on top of the clock, was Godpapa Drosselmeir! His head was sticking out like the owl's, and his arms in his brown coat hung down like wings. He flapped them as if he wanted to fly but couldn't leave his perch.

Perhaps stranger still was the fact that every object in the room, from the Christmas tree to the smallest of packages under that tree, had grown to an enormous size.

Clara was fascinated! She opened her mouth to call out to Godpapa Drosselmeir, but before she could say a word, she saw such an amazing thing. Oodles of mice in ball gowns and black tuxedos came scampering out of the holes in the walls. The female mice were holding flower petals, dropping them as they skipped into the room. The males looked more royal. They had little canes that they waved around as they danced to music. All the mice were squeaking so loudly, Clara had to cover her ears.

She tried to shout above them to Godpapa Drosselmeir, but something from below her startled her. She looked down at her feet. Coming out of the floor was the king of all the mice. He had a silver sword that flashed as he waved it in the air. Much to Clara's horror, the king had seven horrible heads, each one wearing a tiny crown. His fourteen little eyes shifted to look around the room. But they all kept coming back to glare at the little girl.

The army of mice began to form lines behind their king. Thousands of them appeared. Clara was so frightened that she moved a chair over to the toy cupboard and climbed quickly to the top. But this did her no good. The mice began marching right up the side of the cupboard, their sights set on Clara.

The young girl squirmed, trying to figure out how to escape. She tried to look around for a safer place to hide. She kicked her feet wildly, not knowing what else to do. As she swung them around, she broke the piece of glass on the front of the cupboard door! Her mother and father always warned her not to get too close to the cupboard for this reason. They always asked her to be careful when playing indoors. But this was purely an accident. At the moment, Clara wished her mother would come in to scold her. At least Mother would be able to help her.

The falling glass was exactly what Clara needed, however. It sent the mice scampering and squeaking back to the holes and cracks in the wall.

Clara didn't even have time to sigh in relief. A loud sound, like something being pushed over the floor and people shouting startled her. The toys were gathering together! Soldiers, puppets, dolls, and candy people—they all ran around the drawing room.

It was a total madhouse! Then the nutcracker leaped out from Miss Claire's bed and called the toys to attention. The army quickly formed rows and stopped their noise. Now the mice, also responding to the nutcracker's call, came out from their holes carrying bows and arrows. They fell into many rows and stood opposite the toys. They squeaked a chant that frightened Clara.

"We are mice, we are strong, we can fight you all night long!"

There was going to be a battle between the two groups! The toy army brought out cannons that shot sugarplums, and guns that shot nuts. They fired their weapons over and over at the mice. But the rows of mice seemed endless. As soon as one rank fell, a new one would appear. They shot their arrows one after another, knocking the toys down. There were so many mice in the room, the toys were being defeated.

Clara watched in horror as the toy army got smaller and smaller. Three bold mice began to attack the nutcracker.

"Oh, my poor nutcracker!" Clara called. Her

gift, the thing she loved most in the world, was in danger. She took off her shoe and threw it as hard as she could, aiming for the king of mice.

At that second, the mice disappeared. Clara didn't know if she hit the king. Had she managed to make them all go away by throwing her shoe? All she knew was . . . they were gone.

She heard the distant voice of the nutcracker say, "Clara, you have saved my life. For that, I will love you forever."

"Nutcracker?" she asked, looking about the room. "Nutcracker . . . ?"

"It is Prince Nutcracker now," the young man said, stepping out of the darkness.

Clara turned around to see a handsome prince. He reminded her very much of God-papa Drosselmeir's nephew whom she had met earlier.

"I am from the Land of Sweets, a place where the trees are sugarcoated and the houses drip with frosting. It is every child's dream to go there," the prince said with a smile.

"But how . . . ?" Clara started again, very confused by the evening she was having.

"You helped me defeat the king of mice and his army before he took over the Land of Sweets. Which now makes you the princess of the land. Come, let me show you."

The gentle prince took her hand. He led her behind a grove of trees and into a world like no other. Snowflakes glistened like sugar as they fell softly from the sky. Clara couldn't resist the joy of catching one on her tongue.

"It's lovely here!" she whispered while a smile spread across her face. Every inch of the land was laced with candy as far as she could see.

A path led them through a forest of Christmas trees, heavy with candy canes and peppermint sticks. To the right, there was a river of chocolate with candy bar benches along the shores.

Peanut butter blossoms and sugar-rolled cherries dotted the hedges.

"I see a boat!" Clara clapped with excitement. She almost forgot she was now a princess.

A glass boat sailed right up to the waiting couple. It was beautiful! The boat reflected the colors of every sweet thing around it.

Clara was so dazzled by the colorful boat that she barely noticed the passenger on board.

"This is the Sugar Plum Fairy," the prince told Clara. "She looks after the kingdom while I am away."

Clara smiled shyly. She had never seen anyone so lovely. The fairy's gown was very long. It had pearls, lace, and silk that seemed to trail on forever. Once the fairy stepped off the boat, her gown opened at the bottom—and out came a parade of little dancers!

First there were Spanish dancers, who presented the prince and princess with steaming hot cocoa. An Arabian dancer, whose silks were dark like coffee, moved her arms in wide majestic circles. Three Chinese dancers performed a lighthearted number that made Clara laugh. They did splits in the air and sprinkled loose leaves of tea over the ground. Then a troop of Russian soldiers stepped to a lively beat. Some peppermint sticks, gumdrops, taffy, and bonbons followed in a swirling dance. The Sugar Plum Fairy finished with a graceful duet with her handsome cavalier.

The dances enchanted Clara so much that she almost forgot she was sitting next to her nutcracker prince. She smiled and thanked him for bringing her to the Land of Sweets.

The hours passed like minutes until eventually it was time to return. Clara stepped into a sleigh that would take her home. She couldn't believe all that she had seen this Christmas Eve. The young girl had experienced enough sweet memories to last forever. With her prince beside her, and a bag of gumdrops in her lap, Clara took off into the sky.

∝

"Clara . . . sweetheart, it's time to get up! It's Christmas morning!" At her mother's words, she opened her eyes. Clara was in her mother's bed, Miss Claire beside her.

"Oh, Mother," Clara said, realizing where she was, "I am a princess now! I've been to the Land of Sweets. And there was a terrible fight between the mice and the toys! I helped . . . !" Her words trailed off.

"You must have been dreaming, my dear Clara," her mother said with a smile. "I found you sleeping under the Christmas tree with the nutcracker lying next to you."

"My nutcracker!" Clara cried. "Where is he?"

She looked around the room in a panic. "My prince! Are you here?" Clara's mother took the nutcracker from her dresser and placed it in Clara's hand.

"Here is your funny little man. Godpapa Drosselmeir and his nephew came by early this morning and fixed his teeth and jaw. He is as good as new!"

She hugged him then placed him on the pillow beside her. It had been a wonderful Christmas! Even after all the dolls, dresses, and toys Clara received, the nutcracker was her favorite gift. She could never imagine celebrating a Christmas without him. As long as she had him, she would always be reminded of her sweet adventure.

"Thank you, my prince," she whispered into the nutcracker's ear. "For this, I will love you forever."

What Do *You* Think?
Questions for Discussion

❧

Have you ever been around a toddler who keeps asking the question "Why?" Does your teacher call on you in class with questions from your homework? Do your parents ask you questions about your day at the dinner table? We are always surrounded by questions that need a specific response. But is it possible to have a question with no right answer?

The following questions are about the book you just read. But this is not a quiz! They are designed to help you look at the people, places, and events in the story from different angles. These questions do not have specific answers. Instead, they might make you think of the story in a completely new way.

Think carefully about each question and enjoy discovering more about this classic story.

1. Cinderella's fairy godmother grants her wish to go to the prince's ball by giving her a golden carriage, six horses, one coachman, six footmen, and a beautiful gown. Do you think this is everything Cinderella needs? If you were the fairy godmother, what might be one more thing you would do for Cinderella?

2. How does the prince find Aurora hidden behind the wall of thorns and vines? Why couldn't other princes find her? Do you think Aurora and this prince were always meant to be together?

3. Sleeping Beauty and Cinderella both

marry princes at the end of their stories. Can you imagine a royal wedding? What would it be like?

4. "Why, you are just a doll!" Swanilda exclaims when she finds out Coppélia is not a real girl. Is she just a doll, or is she something more? Why do you think Coppélius made her?

5. Queen Odette is a swan every day until the clock strikes midnight. If you were to turn into an animal every day, which animal would it be? Why?

6. Becoming human meant that the Little Mermaid had to leave behind her home in the ocean. How would you feel if you had to give up the life you knew? Would you have done the same thing to get something you truly wanted?

7. Did you feel sorry for the Ugly Duckling throughout the story? What would you want to say to cheer him up?

8. The firebird gives the prince a feather of his in exchange for his freedom. He tells the prince

that the feather might save his life someday. Did it? Do you own an object that could be considered a lucky charm?

9. Clara Stahlbaum loves the nutcracker more than any other gift she receives. What is your favorite gift you received at Christmas?

10. Prince Nutcracker is from the Land of Sweets, "a place where the trees are sugarcoated and the houses drip with frosting." He says it is every child's dream to go there. Is that your dream place? What is your favorite part of the Land of Sweets?

A Note to Parents and Educators
By Arthur Pober, EdD

✧

First impressions are important.

Whether we are meeting new people, going to new places, or picking up a book unknown to us, first impressions count for a lot. They can lead to warm, lasting memories or can make us shy away from any future encounters.

Can you recall your own first impressions and earliest memories of reading the classics?

Do you remember wading through pages and pages of text to prepare for an exam? Or were you the child who hid under the blanket to read with a flashlight, joining forces with Robin Hood to save Maid Marian? Do you remember only how long it took you to read a lengthy novel such as *Little Women*? Or did you become best friends with the March sisters?

Even for a gifted young reader, getting through long chapters with dense language can easily become overwhelming and can obscure the richness of the story and its characters. Reading an abridged, newly crafted version of a classic novel can be the gentle introduction a child needs to explore the characters and story-line without the frustration of difficult vocabulary and complex themes.

Reading an abridged version of a classic novel gives the young reader a sense of independence and the satisfaction of finishing a "grown-up" book. And when a child is engaged with and inspired by a classic story, the tone is set for further exploration of the story's themes, characters, history, and details. As a child's reading skills advance, the desire to tackle the original, unabridged version of the story will naturally emerge.

If made accessible to young readers, these stories can become invaluable tools for understanding themselves in the context of their families and social environments. This is why the Classic Starts series includes questions that stimulate discussion regarding the impact and social relevance of the characters and stories today. These questions can foster lively conversations between children and their parents or teachers. When we look at the issues, values, and standards of past times in terms of how we live now, we can appreciate literature's classic tales in a very personal and engaging way.

Share your love of reading the classics with a young child, and introduce an imaginary world real enough to last a lifetime.

Dr. Arthur Pober, EdD

Dr. Arthur Pober has spent more than twenty years in the fields of early childhood and gifted education. He is the former principal of one of the world's oldest laboratory schools for gifted youngsters, Hunter College Elementary School, and former Director of Magnet Schools for the Gifted and Talented for more than 25,000 youngsters in New York City.

Dr. Pober is a recognized authority in the areas of media and child protection and is currently the U.S. representative to the European Institute for the Media and European Advertising Standards Alliance.

Explore these wonderful stories in our
Classic Starts™ library.